Prologue

Near Tromso, Norway, so f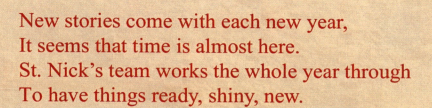
It's still quite cool July the
Up in this freezing artic dome
St. Nick and his team make their home.

New stories come with each new year,
It seems that time is almost here.
St. Nick's team works the whole year through
To have things ready, shiny, new.

In '46 it fell apart
'Till Yorkshire's dogs all played their part
And helped make sure the toys got there
To all the children everywhere.

A great world war had just gone down
But small ones now were all around.
Nick knew again he'd have to weave
Together ceasefires Christmas Eve.

The New Year's guests had left for home.
Zoe was back from friends in Rome.
Now he would tell her in his way
How the Yorkies saved the day.

- Two whole weeks since he'd seen Zoe,
Lots of news - plus - little Stowie!

"Welcome home! I'm glad to see you!
Here's a surprise - and lots of news."
Zoe hugged her husband tightly,
Reached for Stowie, smiling brightly.

"He saw his chance and stowed away
Beneath the blankets in the sleigh.
The elves found him to their surprise,
And they all loved his yellow eyes."

Nick didn't know, but he could guess,
Stowie's childhood's been a mess.

He's never had a place to sleep,
Except outside, the cold bone-deep.
His only food from York's trash bins,
And not a single human friend.

When Zoe was away in Rome,
Stowie'd made himself at home.
She knit with yarns and knit with thread,
Looked up and Stowie's on the bed.

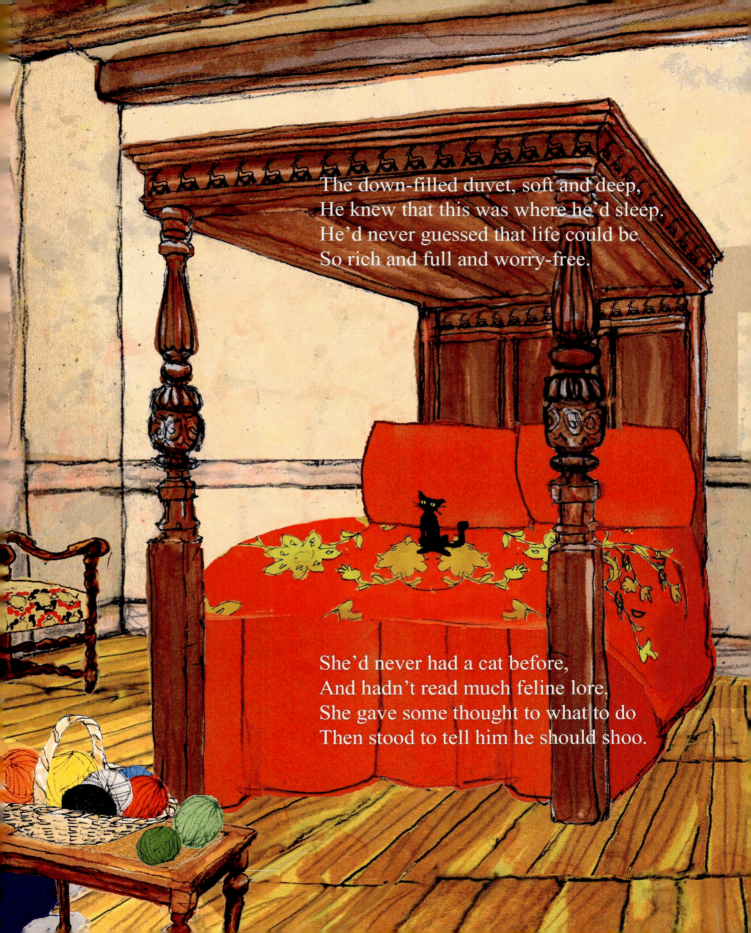

The down-filled duvet, soft and deep,
He knew that this was where he'd sleep.
He'd never guessed that life could be
So rich and full and worry-free.

She'd never had a cat before,
And hadn't read much feline lore.
She gave some thought to what to do
Then stood to tell him he should shoo.

This sleeping place, he'd never leave.
Zoe'd have to get past her peeve.

So, he ignored her, licked his paw.
She stifled laughter, but he saw.
Thereafter Stowie came and went
Just as he chose, with her assent.

Stowie ambled through the house.
He spied a blur - a little mouse.

He chased the mouse for quite a while,
and slipped and skidded on the tile.
At last by chance he caught its tail.
The mouse let out a little wail.

"That little mouse won't hurt a thing.
You let him go, good things he'll bring."
Stowie stopped and gave it thought -
He knew that friends could not be bought.

"He's really small, I will admit.
He's just a teensy little bit."
He felt a twinge, but let him go
And gained a friend, the best he'd know.

"Make sure you have new summer clothes,
We're going south where warm breeze flows.
Sea plane's chartered, it's terrific!
This year's trip's to the Pacific!"

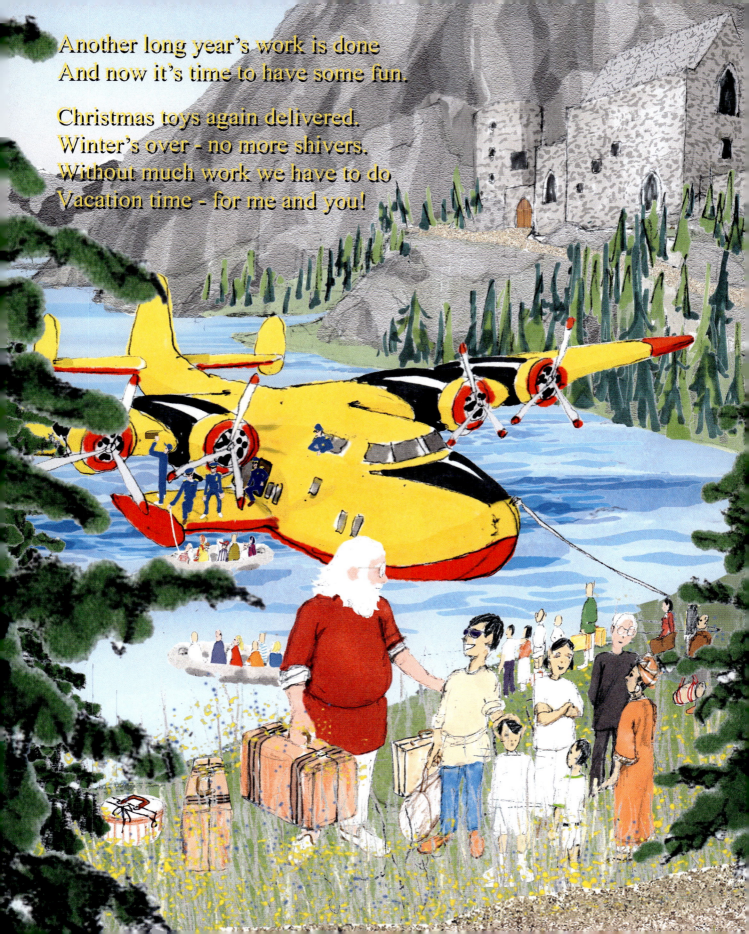

Another long year's work is done
And now it's time to have some fun.

Christmas toys again delivered.
Winter's over - no more shivers.
Without much work we have to do
Vacation time - for me and you!

A growing roar, the great plane cleaved
The water's surface, then it heaved
Into the air, and reached up high
Into the great Norwegian sky.

A long but fun and perfect flight,
The sun is warm, the breeze is light.
A two-week break from work and care,
Hawaiian music's in the air!

With wind and surf, the tall trees sway
And weighty thoughts all fade away.
It's time to launch the long canoe
Onto the ocean, bright and blue.

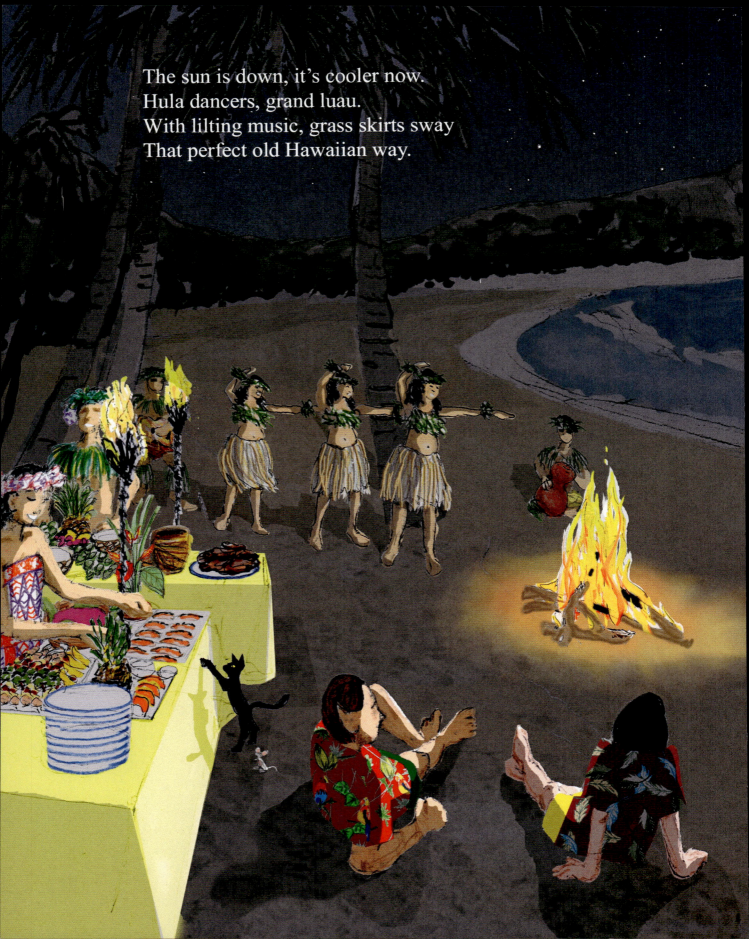

The sun is down, it's cooler now.
Hula dancers, grand luau.
With lilting music, grass skirts sway
That perfect old Hawaiian way.

A grumpy kitten, calico
Crept to the edge of campfire glow.
She heard the music, smelled the food.
All this improved the kitten's mood.

When Zoe asked the luau crew
Where kitten came from, no one knew.
"We can't just leave her here alone."
She asked if she could take her home.

With tiny luau cat on board,
The plane, fueled up, provisions stored,
Takes off, begins its Northern run.
This grand vacation, so much fun!

Gentle kitten, colors alight,
Brightens the mood for the whole flight.
The children laugh, the grownups smile.
The name "Maui" wins by a mile!

"An earring's lost. It can't be found,
I've looked and looked, just all around.
It was here yesterday at lunch.
I left it here, now have no hunch.

"Nick gave them to me long ago.
I know I'll find it, I just know!"

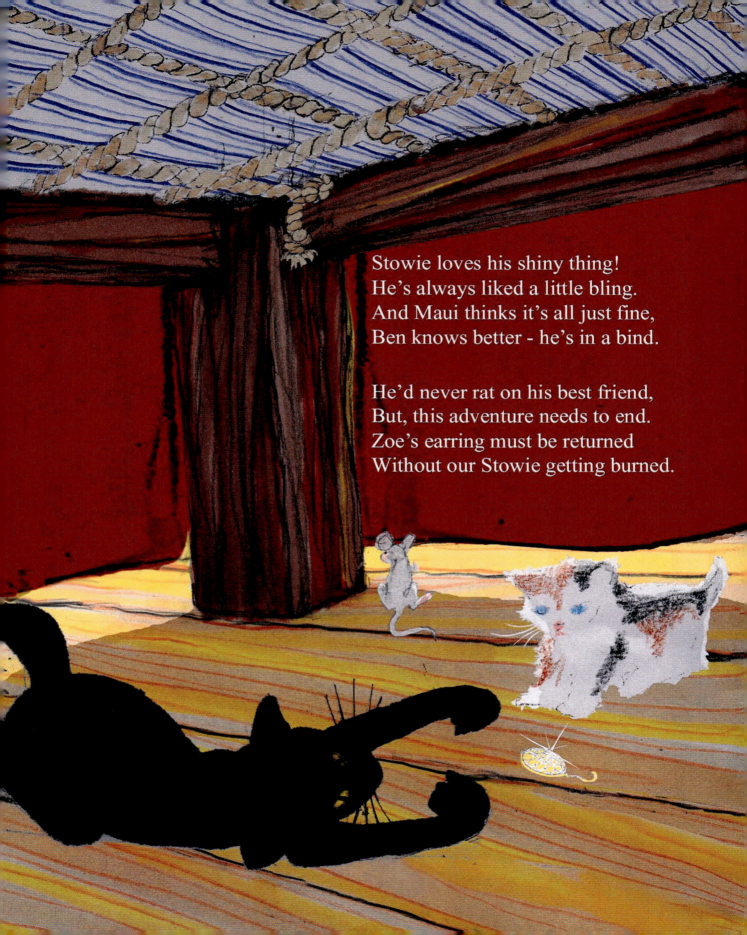

Stowie loves his shiny thing!
He's always liked a little bling.
And Maui thinks it's all just fine,
Ben knows better - he's in a bind.

He'd never rat on his best friend,
But, this adventure needs to end.
Zoe's earring must be returned
Without our Stowie getting burned.

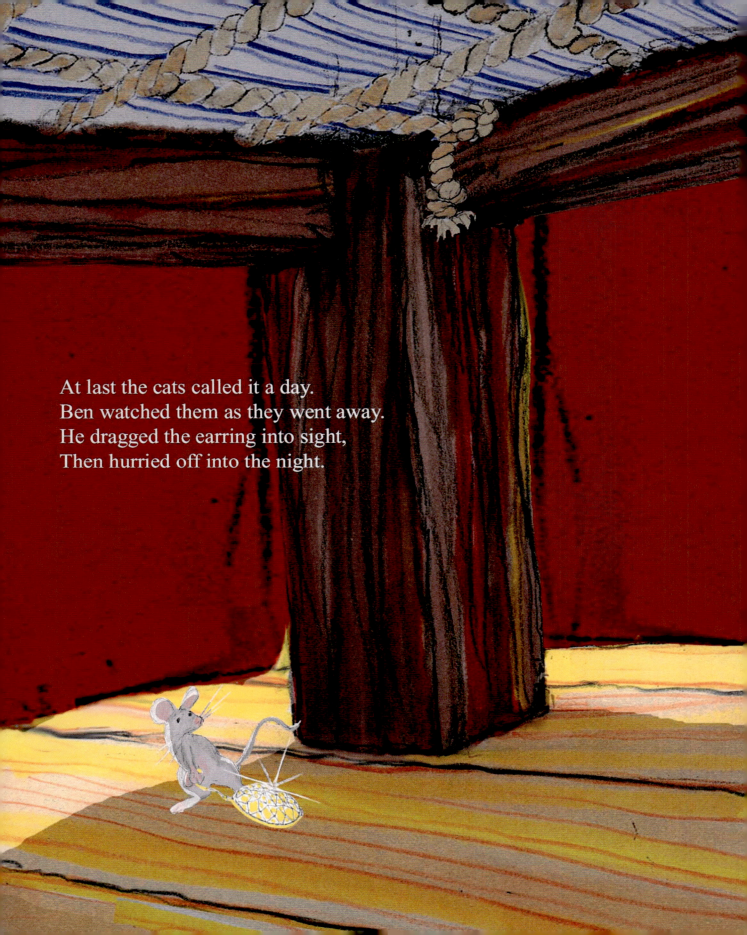

At last the cats called it a day.
Ben watched them as they went away.
He dragged the earring into sight,
Then hurried off into the night.

The elders of the Elves all came
To Tromso to discuss, again
The safety of the childrens' homes
Wherever armies went to roam.

They talked of many other things,
Cheered up by knowing Christmas brings
Great joy to children ev'rywhere,
No other time could quite compare!

The president saw no problem.
"You need ceasefires, you will get 'em.
These wars are awful, large and small,
And Chrismas spirit blesses all."

Now tons of mail arrive each day
And hundreds make the lists that say
Who wants what, and where it goes
The night St. Nick's team always shows
That children's dreams are so worthwhile.
The whole world loves to see them smile.

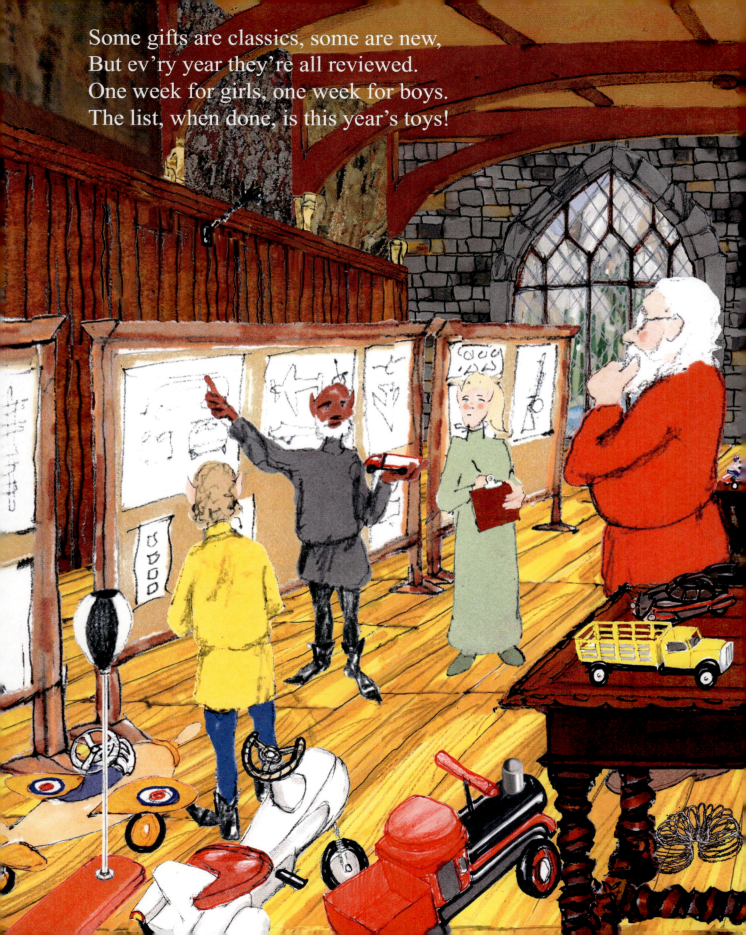

Some gifts are classics, some are new,
But ev'ry year they're all reviewed.
One week for girls, one week for boys.
The list, when done, is this year's toys!

In Tromso's cave are wizards' arts,
They know physics from stars to quarks.
Travel dust keeps the sleighs aloft,
They take off hard, but land so soft.

Right now they're trying to improve
The way the warp drive finds its groove.
Nick uses wormholes for great speed.
The way that works is quite a read.

Tomorrow morning, eyes will gleam
For presents left by St Nick's team.
This cold Christmas Eve it's fitting -
The new scarf of Zoey's knitting.

It's time to head to the North Pole
And start to play their yearly role.
A trusty team of strong reindeer -
Who'll have a backup team this year!

Polar base is ready and packed.
Torches lit and packages stacked.
Ready to close the year out right,
- All the gifts delivered tonight.

It takes eight months, very few know
To take the gifts through cold and snow
In one night's time, by earthly clocks.
Einstein and Elvish picked time's locks.

It had been a very good year,
Friends invited from far and near.
As they came in, Nick thanked each one
For being friends; for what they'd done.

They'd come to Tromso, honored guests
They'd all helped Christmas be its best.
Ike and Mamie, Harry and Bess,
De Gaulle, Churchill, and all the rest.

Unlikely friends? You'd think to say?
It matters not, this Christmas Day.
In any season, any day,
Goodwill and friendship find the way.

Also by Russell Claxton

THE ST. NICHOLAS YORKIES
SAVING CHRISTMAS DAY

A Christmas tale of near-disaster, and a spirited response from the people and dogs of York.

The story will probably delight anyone who's ever known a dog.

Or a reindeer.

Or a cat.

THE ST. NICHOLAS OWLS
AND THE LUCKIEST LAB

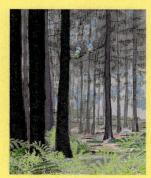

From a pair of unearthly eggs to a sharp-eyed rescue, the owls bring a new dimension to the St. Nicholas team in Tromso, and a new Labrador puppy.

ST. NICHOLAS IN PARIS
PRESIDENTS, POODLES, AND PARADES

1959. An invitation from the president of France brings St. Nick and the whole team to Paris for a visit, the Carnival, and a state dinner in appreciation for his work.

There were some surprises, too.

ST. NICHOLAS AND THE DOGS OF ROME

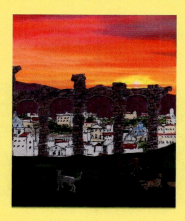

1954. Eight years after recruiting 44 Yorkies to save Christmas Day, Sally is going to college with a scholarship in Rome. She continues a new-found interest in rescuing dogs along with her studies.

www.blueigloobooks.com

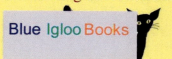

About the author

Russell Claxton, a Texas native, has called Macon, Georgia home for over twenty-five years with his wife Natalie and a string of dogs, cats and wildlife.

He is a practicing architect and urban designer. The conservation of natural resources runs high on his list of priorities.

Animal well-being is a life-long preoccupation, with accompanying enjoyment and appreciation of dogs, cats and lots of other animal friends.

Made in the USA
Columbia, SC
14 August 2022